Gripper, G
and the Sports

Illustrations by Nigel Chilvers

EGMONT

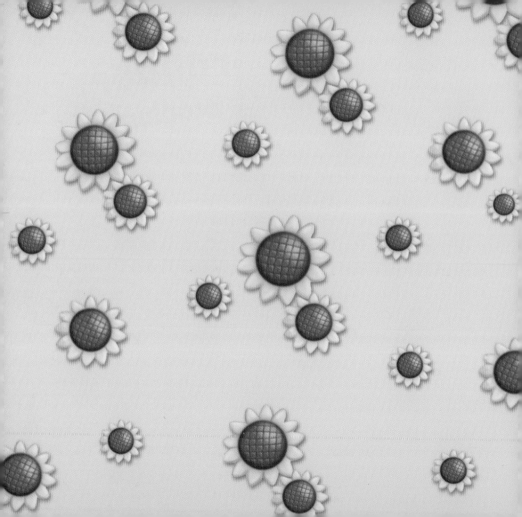

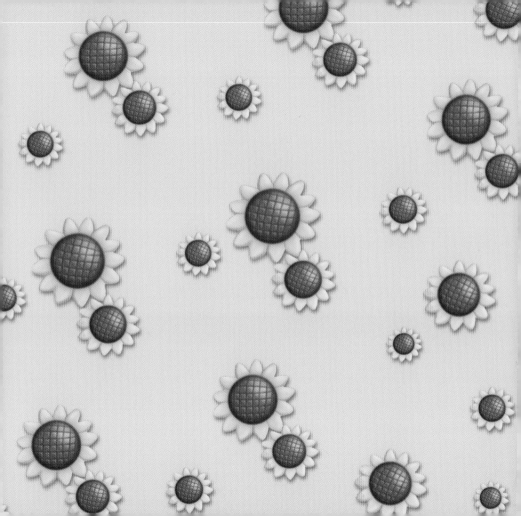

EGMONT

We bring stories to life

First published in Great Britain 2009 by Egmont UK Limited
The Yellow Building, 1 Nicholas Road, London W11 4AN

Endpapers and introductory illustrations by Craig Cameron.

ISBN 978 1 4052 4627 9

46326/2

Printed in Italy

Egmont is passionate about helping to preserve the world's remaining ancient forests.
We only use paper from legal and sustainable forest sources.

This book is made from paper certified by the Forest Stewardship Council® (FSC®),
an organisation dedicated to promoting responsible management of forest resources.
For more information on the FSC, please visit www.fsc.org. To learn more about
Egmont's sustainable paper policy, please visit www.egmont.co.uk/ethical

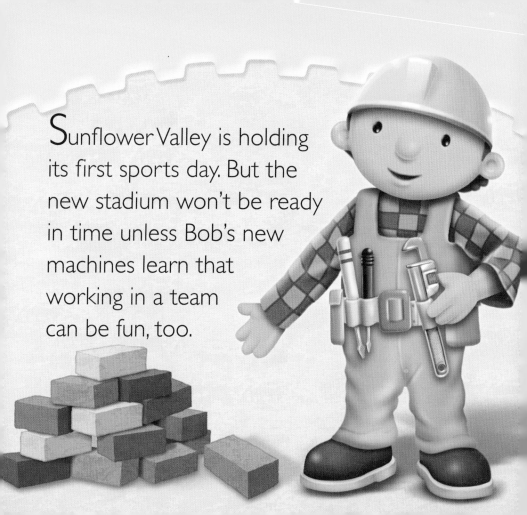

Sunflower Valley is holding its first sports day. But the new stadium won't be ready in time unless Bob's new machines learn that working in a team can be fun, too.

One fine day in Sunflower Valley, everyone had gathered to listen to Mr Bentley.

"I am delighted to announce the very first Sunflower Valley Games," he said, grandly, and everyone cheered.

"You love sports, Wendy! Will you join in?" said Dizzy, excitedly.

"We'll be busy building the stadium," said Wendy. "But Scrambler said he'd help me to train for the Games after work."

Just then, there came a rumbling sound. Bob's machines looked at each other nervously. Suddenly, two huge bulldozers with caterpillar tracks rolled into view.

"Aha, our new team-mates are here," smiled Bob. "Their special tracks help them to move materials, even in mud!"

"He's Gripper," said one.

"He's Grabber!" said the other.

"We work together," they said, grinning.

Later, at the stadium building site, Bob and the team all got down to work. All except Gripper and Grabber, that is.

"Hey, mate, let's go and explore," said Gripper. "Just us, Gripper and Grabber!"

"You bet!" Grabber said. "Grabber and Gripper. Let's have some fun together."

"W-wait, we need your help!" said Scoop. But it was too late, the big machines had rumbled off into the woods.

Gripper and Grabber were exploring the woods when Gripper spotted a rabbit.

"Gripper, where are you?" called Grabber. But there was no reply. "He's zoomed off without me! I'd better go back," he sniffed.

Meanwhile, Gripper had lost the rabbit . . . and Grabber too! "Grabber's left me behind!" he said, sadly.

Gripper and Grabber were worried. They were not used to being on their own.

Grabber trundled back to the site, where Bob's team was working happily.

Suddenly, Lofty moaned, "Help, this girder's too heavy, I can't control it!"

The giant girder moved this way and that. As it swung back towards Lofty's face, Grabber's bucket stopped it, just in time.

"Phew! Thanks, Grabber," said Lofty.

"It's too heavy for you. Gripper should have been here to lift it," sighed Grabber.

Poor Grabber was missing his friend. When work was finished for the day, he set off to find him. He wanted them to build the sports stadium together.

Meanwhile, Gripper was still trying to find his way back. It was getting dark and there were lots of strange noises. "I wish Grabber were here," he sighed.

Suddenly, there was a loud CRASH! The two friends had bumped into each other.

"Ouch!" As Grabber backed away from Gripper, his caterpillar wheels slipped over the edge of the cliff. Gripper swung his hook and just caught Grabber.

"Hold on, mate," shouted Gripper, pulling as hard as he could.

"Help me!" called Grabber but it was no good, Gripper couldn't pull Grabber up.

"We're stuck. Let's hope someone looks for us soon," he called to Grabber.

Next morning, Bob noticed Grabber and Gripper weren't there. "They may be in trouble, we'd better find them," he said.

The team followed the tracks towards the mountain path. Suddenly, they saw Gripper at the cliff edge.

"Help!" he cried, "Grabber's gone over the edge. I can't hold on much longer."

"Hold on! Wendy's been training, she can throw a rope around him," shouted Bob.

Wendy threw the rope as hard as she could. It flew through the air and looped round Gripper's cab.

"Hurray!" the team shouted. They pulled on the rope, and slowly, Gripper and the machines lifted Grabber on to the path.

"Well done, team," said Bob. "Now, we've a stadium to finish – fast! Can we build it?"

"Yes, we can!" shouted the team.

"Er, yeah, I think so," added Lofty.

The team worked hard to finish the stadium. The day of the Sunflower Valley Games had arrived. Everyone was waiting for the first event, the heptathlon.

"What's a hep . . . er, hefa-lon?" asked Roley.

"It's a competition of seven sports," laughed Bob. "Wendy's trained hard."

The crowd cheered loudly as Wendy ran and jumped and threw her way through all seven events . . .

"Wendy wins the gold medal," yelled Mr Bentley. "And now – the race we've all been waiting for – the Machine Relay!"

BANG! The starting gun popped and the machines were away. Lofty passed the baton to Scoop, then Scoop zoomed to Dizzy, who raced towards Grabber. Then Gripper snatched it up with his hook and raced over the winning line.

Bob's team had won!

"Well done, team," beamed Bob. "Super teamwork! It's gold medals all round!"

"Wow, that was great!" said Grabber.

"The reason we won is because we were part of a team. We've had lots of fun working together," said Gripper.

"And now it's time to play together, let's celebrate!" smiled Grabber.

"Welcome to the team!" chuckled Bob.

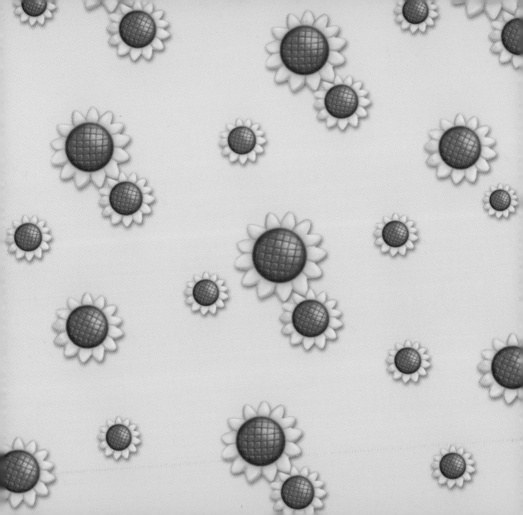

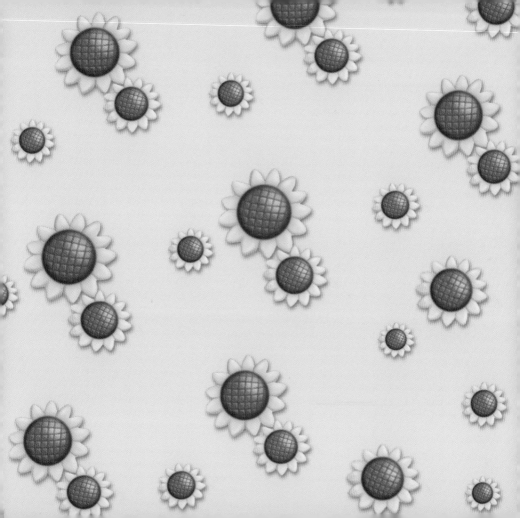

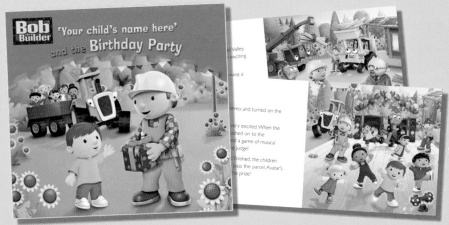